ONE, TWO, BUCKLE MY SHOE

Retold by STEVEN ANDERSON

Illustrated by TAKAKO FISHER

CANTATA
LEARNING

MANKATO, MINNESOTA

WWW.CANTATALEARNING.COM

CANTATA
LEARNING
MANKATO, MINNESOTA

Published by Cantata Learning
1710 Roe Crest Drive
North Mankato, MN 56003
www.cantatalearning.com

Library of Congress Control Number: 2014957027
978-1-63290-287-0 (hardcover/CD)
978-1-63290-439-3 (paperback/CD)
978-1-63290-481-2 (paperback)

One, Two, Buckle My Shoe by Steven Anderson
Illustrated by Takako Fisher

Book design, Tim Palin Creative
Editorial direction, Flat Sole Studio
Executive musical production and direction, Elizabeth Draper
Music arranged and produced by Steven C Music

Printed in the United States of America.

VISIT
WWW.CANTATALEARNING.COM/ACCESS-OUR-MUSIC
TO SING ALONG TO THE SONG

Practice counting as you sing along

to this classic Mother Goose rhyme!

Now turn the page, and sing along.

One, two, **buckle** my shoe.

Three, four, shut the door.

Five, six, pick up sticks.

Seven, eight, lay them straight.

Nine, ten, do it again!

One, two, buckle my shoe.

Three, four, open the door.

Five, six, pick up sticks.

Seven, eight, lay them straight.

Nine, ten, do it again!

SONG LYRICS
One, Two, Buckle My Shoe

One, two, buckle my shoe.

Three, four, shut the door.

Five, six, pick up sticks.

Seven, eight, lay them straight.

Nine, ten, do it again!

One, two, buckle my shoe.
Three, four, open the door.

Five, six, pick up sticks.
Seven, eight, lay them straight.

Nine, ten, do it again!

One, Two, Buckle My Shoe

(instrumental)

Verse 2
One, two, buckle my shoe.
Three, four, open the door.
Five, six, pick up sticks.
Seven, eight, lay them straight.
Nine, ten, do it again!

GLOSSARY

buckle—to close a shoe by fastening it with a strap and a metal clasp

GUIDED READING ACTIVITIES

1. Read through this story again. Make new rhymes as you count to ten.

2. What words rhyme in this story?

3. Who is the illustrator of this story? What does an illustrator do?

TO LEARN MORE

Cabrera, Jane. *One, Two, Buckle My Shoe*. New York: Holiday House, 2009.

Crews, Donald. *Ten Black Dots*. New York: HarperCollins, 2009.

Nunn, Daniel. *Counting 1 to 10*. Mankato, MN: Capstone Press, 2013.

Rissman, Rebecca. *Counting at Home*. Mankato, MN: Capstone Press, 2013